TWISTAPLOT®

13

Midnight at Monster Mansion

Steven Otfinoski

Illustrations by Michael Racz

SCHOLASTIC INC.
New York Toronto London Auckland Sydney

To Daniel,
the little monster in our mansion.

ISBN 0-590-33230-9

12 11 10 9 8 7 6 5   8/8

Printed in the U.S.A.   01

BEWARE!!!
DO NOT READ THIS BOOK FROM BEGINNING TO END

Y ou are about to enter a house of countless horrors where your worst nightmares will come true. Read the directions at the bottom of each page carefully. Take your time before turning each page. A different terror lurks behind every door and in each shadow. The slightest misstep could mean instant death . . . or worse!

But don't despair. If you are clever, courageous, or just plain lucky, you may survive the long, dark night in this house of monsters and see the light of day once more.

So take a deep breath and brace yourself for what lies ahead. Bloodthirsty vampires, howling werewolves, powerful zombies, and Frankenstein's Monster himself await your arrival. . . .

Go on to PAGE 2.

What a great vacation! You have been visiting some friends who have a summer house at the beach, and now you're driving home in your father's new sports car, which he finally agreed to lend you for the trip.

It's a long drive and you decide to try a shortcut on a back road. Bad decision! Soon you're hopelessly lost. You look for a place to stop and ask directions, but there isn't a house or building in sight.

That's not your only problem. You've been listening to the radio when you should have been paying attention to the gas gauge. The needle is on empty! Will you make it to a gas station before you run out? Your chances don't look good.

All at once you hear a deep rumble in the sky. You look up and see storm clouds gathering overhead. That's all you need! To be stranded in the middle of nowhere is bad enough. But in a thunderstorm? You begin to wish you had stayed on the main highway. Better to get home an hour later than not get there at all, you think to yourself as the first raindrops hit the car roof.

Turn to PAGE 4.

Suddenly you see a house up ahead on the right. It is a large, ramshackle mansion set on a small hill. The house is dark and gloomy and looks about a hundred years old. It reminds you of a house you saw in a horror movie on *The Late, Late Show* last week.

A flash of lightning crackles above the mansion, bathing the old house in an eerie glow. You feel cold shivers run down your spine.

You don't like the idea of going up to that house, but you also don't want to spend the night in your father's car during a thunderstorm. If someone is home at the house, you can ask to use the phone and call a gas station for help.

Then again, if there's one house, maybe you'll pass more houses—ones that look less creepy. That is, if you don't run out of gas first. What are you going to do? You'd better make up your mind quickly. The driveway to the mansion is coming up fast.

If you decide to keep going and take your chances on the road, turn to PAGE 87.

If you choose to stop and see if anyone is home, turn to PAGE 6.

You give the hunchback your brightest, bravest smile and step inside. The main hall is filled with heavy, old-fashioned furniture. You notice cobwebs everywhere. But the fire is warm and that's the important thing.

"Wait here," says the hunchback, closing the door. In a moment, a tall, distinguished-looking gentleman in a black cape and evening clothes enters with the servant.

"Ah!" he says in a thick foreign accent. "You're here at last! I trust your drive wasn't too difficult. I am Dr. Alucard and this is my servant, Igor."

Igor! It figures—right out of an old horror movie. And Alucard? That name sounds familiar, too.

"Please take off your jacket and I will bring you to the patient at once. We have no time to lose," Alucard says.

Patient? You thought *he* was the doctor! Not that he looks like one. Maybe it's time you told these people just who you really are before you get into deep trouble. Of course, they may throw you back out in the storm if you do.

If you decide to set this Alucard character straight right now, turn to PAGE 9.

If you decide to play along awhile longer, turn to PAGE 11.

6

You drive up the long, twisting driveway. The house looks even creepier up close. The worn shutters are all closed, but you can see light downstairs. Someone must be home. You park the car and carefully lock it. (Your father would kill you if anything happened to it!)

Slowly you walk up the front porch steps. They squeak noisily under your feet. You feel your courage draining away, but you raise your fist and rap loudly on the door.

There is a long silence. You knock again. You can hear your heart beating wildly under the noise of the rain and thunder. Finally you hear footsteps approaching. The door swings open and a short, stocky man in a butler's uniform stands before you. He is unshaven. His hair is long and scraggly. And you can't help but notice he has a hunchback. He looks you up and down with beady, brown eyes.

"Well," he says in a low, gruff voice. "It's about time you got here!"

You take a step back, startled. This butler has obviously mistaken you for someone else.

"Don't just stand there, fool!" he exclaims impatiently. "Come in! The Master is waiting!"

Go on to PAGE 7.

If the Master looks anything like his servant, you could do without meeting him. But it's cold and damp out there in the rain, and behind the butler you can see a warm, inviting fire. Should you accept the invitation or run for your car and take your chances on the road ahead?

If you decide to go into the house, turn to PAGE 5.

If you decide to return to your car, turn to PAGE 8.

You mumble something to the hunchback about having the wrong address and turn away from the door. Without looking back, you run through the teeming rain to your car. You fish through your pockets for the keys. Oh, no! They're not there.

You stare through the car window and see them still in the ignition. You've locked yourself out! What a klutz! As you start down the long driveway to the main road, you curse yourself for not having an umbrella. It's going to be a wet walk to the next town. Happy hitchhiking!

THE END

"Dr. Alucard," you begin, "I'm afraid you have mistaken me for someone else."

"What?!" exclaims your host in surprise. "You mean to say you are not the television repairperson Igor called?"

"No, I'm just passing through. My car is almost out of gas and I stopped here hoping to use your phone."

"What a shame!" says Alucard, shaking his head. "Igor and I were so looking forward to watching *King Kong Meets Spider Lady* on *The Late, Late Show* tonight. But I suppose we can watch TV anytime. It is a rare treat to have a guest to entertain. Please make yourself comfortable. I will phone the local gas station for you. Meanwhile, Igor will bring you something to drink. Igor, fetch a glass of your special punch."

You are about to protest, but Dr. Alucard doesn't give you the chance. He is already out of the room. Igor goes grumbling toward the kitchen. You sit down in a large, overstuffed chair, dripping rainwater and feeling nervous. You look out at the raindrops streaking down the windows and wish you were safely home in bed.

Continue reading on PAGE 10 and watch out!

Igor returns with a large glass filled with a reddish liquid that is foaming over the sides of the glass and has steam rising from it. It looks like something you concocted last year in chemistry class.

"Drink this," he says, shoving the glass toward you. "It's an old family recipe."

You take the glass and say, "That's really interesting." You hope he doesn't notice how shaky your voice is.

Igor stands there impatiently, waiting for you to take a sip. "I said drink it!" he commands.

You look into the steaming glass. Could the drink be drugged? Is it poison? Do you dare risk insulting this weird guy by refusing his homemade punch?

If you decide to refuse to drink Igor's punch, turn to PAGE 15.

If you decide to get out of drinking it by dropping the glass and making it look like an accident, turn to PAGE 13.

If you decide to drink the awful stuff and hope for the best, turn to PAGE 48.

You decide to keep your true identity a secret for a while longer and follow Dr. Alucard.

"Well, here it is. It started going on the blink this afternoon and hasn't been the same since." Dr. Alucard is pointing to a large television set. The TV is the "patient" and you have been mistaken for a television repairperson!

Alucard begins to eye you suspiciously for the first time. "You can fix it, can't you?" he asks.

"Sure," you say. You're in this too deep to tell the truth now. You turn on the set, trying to act as professional as possible.

"Look at the colors," says Alucard. "Aren't they a bit odd?"

You stare at the small screen. The bright colors are swirling around like the colored bits of glass in a kaleidoscope. Reds the color of blood. Vivid greens. Disturbing dark blues. Round and round the colors go, hypnotizing you.

You feel your will being sucked right out of your body. You want to tear your eyes away from the diabolical patterns, but you can't. Out of the corner of your eye you spy an ashtray.

___

If you continue to watch the set, turn to PAGE 88.

If you grab the ashtray to smash the screen, turn to PAGE 21.

You would rather let the glass drop to the floor than drink its sickening contents. You let the warm glass slip through your fingers, and it shatters on the floor.

You reach down to pick up some of the pieces of broken glass just as Dr. Alucard returns. A piece of glass cuts your finger. Bright drops of blood ooze out. You look up and see a strange, wild gleam come into the doctor's eyes. He is looking at your cut finger as if he were hypnotized by it. As he approaches, he opens his mouth and two large fangs emerge. Suddenly you realize in horror why the name "Alucard" sounded so familiar. It is "Dracula" spelled backwards! Your host is a vampire!

He begins to suck the blood from your finger. You try to pull away, but his grip holds you. Still thirsty, he goes for your neck. You feel his sharp fangs sink into your skin. You cry out in horror, but soon you give in to the hypnotic spell of Count Dracula. By the end of the night you are a vampire just like Dracula! Don't feel too bad about it, though. After all, you'll live at least a thousand years.

THE END

14

You race down the narrow passageway. Too bad about Frankie. But you did help him once and that was enough.

All at once you notice your feet feel unusually heavy. You look down and see that you have run smack into quicksand. You cry out for help, but unfortunately Frankie is in no condition to assist you. You hear your cries echo off the cavelike walls as the wet sands close over your head.

THE END

"No, I won't drink it," you say flatly.

Igor tries to hide his anger at your refusal. "But you will love it," he exclaims.

"If it's so great, why aren't you drinking any?" you ask him.

Igor growls, showing his rotted teeth. But before he can advance on you, a voice speaks from the doorway.

"It is not nice to refuse refreshment when you are a guest," says Alucard softly.

The quiet, cold tone of his voice frightens you much more than Igor's animal noises.

You turn to face the doctor. His hand is held out to you.

"Come here to me, my friend," he says gently. "There is no reason for you to be afraid. You have come to this house for a purpose. And we must see that the purpose is carried out."

If you want to see what Alucard has in mind, turn to PAGE 37.

If you decide to get the heck out of there, turn to PAGE 19.

You run toward the sound of water and, putting both hands out in front of you, dive in. As you lift your arms to swim, you notice a tingling sensation—a very strong sensation. You look at your arms. They are the arms of a skeleton!

In a matter of seconds, the flesh is eaten from your body and your bones float to the surface. What you mistook for a pool of water was, unfortunately, a pool of acid.

THE END

The sound of voices awakens you. You open your eyes and are immediately blinded by a bright light. You try to move, but can't. You turn your head and see you are strapped down to an operating table.

Igor, dressed now in a white physician's smock, is standing over you. Next to him stands Alucard.

"I must ask you some questions," Dr. Alucard says. "Tell me, how much is two plus two?"

Is he crazy? A math quiz at a time like this? But something tells you from the tense expression on Alucard's face that what happens next depends a lot on what your answer is.

If you decide to answer the question correctly, turn to PAGE 64.

If you decide to play dumb and give the wrong answer, turn to PAGE 20.

You open the door. A short man in jeans and a workshirt stands there.

"Hello," he says. "I'm the TV repairman. I'm sorry it took me so long to get here, but I had this other appointment . . ."

This is no time to chat! You grab his arm and hustle him out the door, closing it behind you. You quickly tell him your terrible story. He looks a little doubtful, but doesn't argue. You notice your car is gone from the driveway, and you don't stop to look for it. The repairman agrees to drive you to the nearest bus station.

As his small van pulls down the gravel driveway, you cast one last look back at the mansion where you almost lost your brain. Your father will be upset about the car, but you figure it's better to lose your allowance for ten years than your life in one night.

THE END

You start to run from the room, knocking over several chairs and a table to block the path of your pursuers. Within seconds you have reached the front door. You seize the doorknob and give it a twist. No good. You're locked in!

From the den you can hear Igor grumbling angrily as he stumbles over the furniture. You look around wildly for another exit.

Before you is a wide, winding staircase leading upstairs. Across the hall is a doorway, probably leading down to the basement. You have only a second to decide which way to go. Only one thing is certain: If you don't make a move quickly, you'll be Alucard's prisoner.

If you choose to take the basement, turn to PAGE 28.

If you choose to go for the staircase, turn to PAGE 30.

"The answer is . . . five?" you reply.

"Wrong!" shoots back Alucard, in great disappointment.

"What is the capital of the United States?" Alucard demands.

"Cleveland," you answer, knowing quite well that it is really Washington, D.C.

"Who invented the car?" shouts Alucard.

"Lee Iacocca," you answer.

"This is terrible!" exclaims the doctor. "Here I thought you were a perfectly intelligent teenager, and now I find out you're an imbecile! I can't place such an inferior brain into the body of my creature!"

So that's it! He wants your brain!

"Igor," screams Alucard, "get him out of here!"

Igor roughly unstraps you from the table and shoves you onto a bed with wheels. He wheels you out of the laboratory and down a long corridor. The floor slants downward slightly. Using your body weight, you could pull away from the hunchback, roll down the corridor, and then leap off the bed and make a break for freedom. It's risky, however, and you may not get far.

If you decide to try to escape now, turn to PAGE 23.

If you choose to wait for a better opportunity, turn to PAGE 86.

You seize the ashtray in your trembling hand and raise it. But before you can hurl it at the evil screen, the colors disappear and an unearthly glow fills the tube. The screen sends out blinding rays of light that freeze you in mid-motion. Every muscle in your body is paralyzed. Your raised hand quivers and you drop the ashtray against your will.

With horror, you feel your whole body being drawn toward the glowing screen. A terrible, tingling sensation comes over you. You want to scream, but you can't move your mouth. You feel as if every molecule of your body is disintegrating.

Suddenly you open your eyes. You see Alucard and Igor standing several feet away, staring down at you. Their bodies are strangely distorted, as if you were looking at them through a mirror or a piece of warped glass. Alucard moves toward you. His hand reaches down for the "off" button on the TV set. Only then do you realize why everything looks so strange. You are *inside* the television set! As Alucard pushes the button, your entire universe goes black. You are a prisoner inside the television . . . forever trapped . . . forever looking out at reality. Happy viewing!

THE END

You open your tired eyes to see sunlight streaming in through a window. It is morning and you are in a small bed.

"He's awake," says a voice nearby. You flinch as you recognize Igor's gruff face. But you are puzzled as the hunchback smiles warmly down at you. By his side is Dr. Alucard, who is also smiling.

"How do you feel?" the doctor asks.

"All right, I guess," you say. "But I don't understand . . ."

"It's all very simple," explains your host. "Igor was driving home last night and found you wandering along the road in the rain, talking to yourself. He brought you here. You were burning with fever and having hallucinations. I gave you some medicine and put you to bed."

"Yes," you say, as it comes back to you. "I remember now. I ran out of gas and was walking along the road, trying to hitch a ride to a gas station."

"Well, now that you feel better, let's go find that car of yours," suggests Alucard.

The doctor and his servant drive you to your car and put enough gas into the tank to get you to a station. You arrive home safely a few hours later with a thrilling story to tell your worried parents. You promise them you'll stick to the beaten track next time!

THE END

It's now or never! You push away from Igor. The bed rolls freely down the corridor. With a bound, you leap off and race around a corner. You can hear Igor's angry cries as you spy a door on your right. You yank it open and step inside. It is a dark closet. You stand there quietly as Igor passes.

Suddenly you are aware that the breathing you hear is not your own. You feel another body brush against yours. Your heart stands still as you see a pair of glowing eyes open and stare into yours from only a few feet away.

If you want to get out of this closet as quickly as possible, turn to PAGE 46.

If you want to stay a little longer, until you are sure it is safe in the corridor, turn to PAGE 50.

"Look what you've done!" cries the vampire. "You've ruined my resting place! For this you will die!"

His hatred for you is so great that he fails to see he is walking into the spreading sunlight. As the light strikes his eyes, he puts up both hands to ward off his doom. But it is too late.

Smoke rises rapidly from his body. You watch with horror as the flesh literally drops from his bones. The screams of the dying vampire fill you with terror, but you continue to watch as if in a trance.

Dracula's charred skeleton clatters to the floor. In another minute, the bones disintegrate into a small pile of dust. Igor enters, takes one look at his Master's remains, and flees.

You go upstairs and find Terry. Together you leave the mansion. Outside the sun is shining brightly. The sky is a vivid blue. Your night of terror seems no more than a bad dream. It is going to be a beautiful day.

THE END

You wake up in darkness. You are lying on a small bed, and your head is throbbing with pain. How long have you been out? You look out the window by your bed and see it is still night, but the storm has passed.

You get up and are relieved to find that only your head is in bad shape. The rest of you seems to be intact. You cross to a wall and feel your way along it until you come to a door. You try the knob and find it unlocked. Just then you hear footsteps approaching. You step back in fear. The footsteps draw closer. Is it Alucard coming to get you? There's no telling what that madman will do to you next! You rush back to the window and open it. The roof slants down below you. It's a long drop to the ground, but you can hide on the roof until Alucard and his servant get tired of looking for you. Later, you can make your escape from inside. The footsteps are nearly at your door. . . .

If you decide to climb out the window, turn to PAGE 89.

If you decide to wait and see if the footsteps go past your door, turn to PAGE 39.

You decide to remain on the roof to find out who this mysterious shadow figure is. From out of the darkness steps a nondescript man. He seems as startled to see you there as you are to see him.

"Oh!" he says nervously. "I thought I was alone."

"What are you doing here?" you ask him.

"I often come out here to be by myself. It's so peaceful and quiet. Are you a new patient of Dr. Alucard's?"

"No," you explain. "I just came here to get help with my car. Alucard is holding me prisoner."

You expect the man to react with surprise, but he merely smiles. "You really shouldn't worry," he says. "The doctor knows what's best. I have complete confidence that he'll cure me of my problem any day now."

"Just what is your problem?" you ask. This fellow doesn't look sick at all.

"It's rather embarrassing," he says, lowering his voice. "You see, I turn into a werewolf every full moon."

You follow his gaze and notice a bright full moon hanging in the night sky!

If you don't believe in werewolves, turn to PAGE 45.

If you do believe in werewolves, turn to PAGE 52.

You remove the key from the wall and unlock the manacles that imprison the monster. He rubs his aching wrists and looks at you with enormous gratitude.

"You help Frankie," he says in a gravelly voice. "You friend."

You shake on it and he nearly crushes every bone in your hand.

"Come," says your new friend. "Me show way out. We leave." That sounds like a great idea to you, and you follow Frankie to a corner of his dungeon. The monster lifts a trap door in the floor and leads you down a steep set of stone stairs.

You are in an underground passage. The only light is from flickering torches hung high on the walls of the passageway. Suddenly Frankie comes to an abrupt halt. He lets out a cry of anguish. Approaching from the other direction are Igor and Alucard. Igor is carrying a large torch, which he waves in Frankie's face. The Monster shrinks back in terror. Fire is the thing he fears most.

The attention of both men is focused on the Monster. You are free to escape down another passageway to the right.

If you decide to leave your friend and run down the passageway, turn to PAGE 14.

If you decide to stay and try to help Frankie, turn to PAGE 55.

You rush to the door and yank it open. Below you stretches a sea of darkness. This is the basement, all right. You take several steps down the stairs and stop to listen.

You hear footsteps rushing up the other staircase. Your pursuers must think that's where you've gone. For the moment you are safe.

You cautiously descend the cellar stairs, not daring to feel for a light switch on the wall. As you reach the cellar floor, you hear the sound of water dripping down a wall. There is a dank, musty smell to the place, like a dungeon.

Suddenly, you hear a low moan from out of the darkness. You are afraid, but your curiosity gets the better of you. You pull a book of matches from your pocket and light one. You hold up the flame in front of you and shudder at the sight it reveals. There, chained to the wall, is the large, hulking figure of . . . Frankenstein's Monster!

Now what do you do? Turn to PAGE 91.

Up the winding staircase you go. You reach the second floor and run down a long hallway past several doors. The last door on the left is closed. You open it and shut it tightly behind you. You listen for footsteps. You hear Igor and his Master go up to the floor above. It's a big mansion and they may not find you for hours, if you keep your wits about you.

You look around the room you have entered. The light of two hanging candles flickers on the wall. At the far end lie two coffins on a small platform. You walk over and examine them. One is made of a greenish stone. The other is cut from wood and is finely polished. What could be inside them?

If you decide to open the wooden coffin, turn to PAGE 33.

If you decide to open the stone coffin, turn to PAGE 34.

If you decide to leave them both alone and check out another room, turn to PAGE 42.

You go to the door where the crying is coming from and try the doorknob. It is locked.

"Who is it?" whispers a frightened voice through the door.

"A friend," you reply.

"Please, get me out of here before he comes back!"

That's all you needed to hear. You brace your shoulder and throw your weight against the door. The old lock breaks away and the door swings open. Standing there is a boy about your age. He is thin and weak.

"How did you get here?" you ask.

"Alucard called the charity I work for, and said he wanted to make a contribution. I came here and was drugged with a drink. I've been his prisoner in this room ever since. My name is Chris."

"Now I see why he called for a TV repairman," you say. "He wanted another victim and mistook me for him."

"Unlucky for you," says Chris grimly. "You know what he has in mind for us, don't you? Alucard's going to use our bodies in his experiments. He's got this monster he's building in a dungeon in the basement. He's almost finished, but all he needs is a brain and a heart. That's where *we* come in."

Turn to PAGE 93.

You are awakened by a crash of thunder. You open your eyes and yawn. Your neck is stiff and your back is sore. You are sitting in the front seat of your father's car, parked by the side of the road. You must have pulled over for a catnap. Dr. Alucard, Igor, the mansion . . . they were all just parts of a crazy dream you had. You sigh with relief and start up the car. The needle on the gas gauge rises to full. Even your car problems were in your dream! You pull back onto the road and turn on your favorite radio station. You casually glance in the rearview mirror just in time to see a figure in a black cape rise up and grab you. His white fangs glisten in the moonlight as your nightmare comes to . . .

THE END

With trembling hands you lift the lid of the wooden coffin. It opens with a creaking sound that sends shivers down your spine. You gasp aloud at the sight inside. It is a girl about your own age. She is dressed in a black cape similar to the one Dr. Alucard wears and has skin so pale it is almost white. Her eyes are closed, as if in a deep sleep. The girl's features are fine and delicate.

As you continue to stare, her eyes slowly open. They are a deep red, the color of blood. The eyes look at you piercingly, as if they could see right through you. Your first impulse is to slam the coffin shut and run. But the beauty of this creature makes you hesistate. Could anyone so beautiful be evil?

If you want to get out of here, turn to PAGE 38.

If you want to stay, turn to PAGE 43.

34

With both hands you lift the lid of the stone coffin. It is heavy and it takes all your strength. You gaze down inside the foul-smelling coffin and shudder. Stretched out before you is a figure wrapped from head to foot in white bandages turned yellow with age. At once you recognize the creature you have seen before only in old horror movies—the Mummy!

Before you can think, the Mummy sits up in his coffin. His moldy arms stretch out for you. You try to move away, but you're paralyzed with fright. The rotting hands seize your throat with supernatural strength. The icy fingers tighten their grip, squeezing the life out of your body.

Go on to PAGE 35.

Just as you are about to fade into unconsciousness, a voice calls out from across the room. "Karla, stop!" it says.

At the sound of the voice, the Mummy's grip on you relaxes and you sink to the floor. You look up and see your rescuer standing in the doorway. It is Dr. Alucard. In his hand he holds a gleaming gold charm. It is fastened to a long chain around his neck. The charm seems to give him power over the Mummy.

"It was not wise of you to leave your room," he tells you. "You were put there for your own protection. It is not safe to wander this house alone."

"I just want to get out of here and go home," you reply.

Alucard places the charm back inside his shirt and smiles. "I'm afraid you will have to stay here a little longer," says your host. "I will have Karla escort you back to your room. I suggest you stay there for the remainder of the evening."

Before Alucard can give his command, you are on your feet. You rush forward. You may not get another chance.

If you want to get the charm from Alucard, turn to PAGE 69.

If you want to get out the door and try to escape, turn to PAGE 75.

Better to take your chances and jump than be ripped to shreds by the Monster. With a cry, you leap off the roof and fall down . . . down . . . down . . . and into the hairy arms of an eight-foot-tall creature. He makes the werewolf on the roof look like a pussycat. As he marches across the front lawn with you, you glance down at his huge feet and realize with a gasp who your captor is—Bigfoot! What a discovery! You are going to be world famous when you prove Bigfoot really exists. Too bad it doesn't work out that way. Bigfoot carries you back to his forest lair and you are never seen or heard from again.

THE END

Alucard stares into your eyes. His eyes are a dark blue. They seem to shine with an unearthly light. You want to turn away, but can't. His eyes have fixed upon yours and you are in their power.

"Come, my friend," says the doctor softly. "There is nothing to be afraid of."

Like a sleepwalker, you move forward at Alucard's command. Igor steps before you and opens a door, but you hardly notice him. You follow your Master obediently into the next room.

"Sit down and relax," he says, pointing to a large chair. You do exactly as he says. There is no other choice.

"Now, close your eyes," Alucard tells you. "Close your eyes and sleep." You do that, too.

What will happen when you wake?

If you're ready for more excitement, turn to PAGE 17

If you've had enough excitement for one night, turn to PAGE 22.

You slam the coffin lid shut on the red-eyed girl inside. Before you can take a step, you hear a sound behind you. You turn and see the lid of the stone coffin slowly opening. Apparently the noise you just made has awakened its occupant. As you stare in horror, a 2,000-year-old Egyptian mummy rises from the coffin. He is trailing dried, yellow bandages behind him. His arms, green with mold, reach out toward you. But luckily, you will never feel the icy grip of those arms. Before the mummy can get you, your heart stops beating and you drop to the floor. You always wondered what it would be like to be scared to death. Now you know.

THE END

You wait and listen, holding your breath. The footsteps are directly outside your door. They pause for a moment and then continue on.

You let out a long sigh of relief. You wait for the footsteps to fade away. Then you open the door very cautiously and look down the darkened hall.

There is not a soul in sight. You quietly step out into the hall and walk down toward a staircase. If you can get to the main floor without being seen, there's a good chance you can find an open door and escape.

Just then you hear a sound coming from behind a door along the hallway. It sounds like someone crying. You stop to listen. Whoever it is sounds very unhappy. But is it any of your concern when your own life may be in danger?

If you decide to investigate, turn to PAGE 31.

If you decide to save your own skin and get down those stairs, turn to PAGE 83.

You turn and start to run for the window. But you never have a chance. The werewolf is on you in seconds! You feel his hot, animal breath on the back of your neck as his clawlike nails dig into your shoulders. He lets out one long, blood-curdling howl and then sinks his teeth into your neck.

Suddenly there is a deafening roar. The werewolf's grip on you relaxes. You watch him go limp and fall dead to the ground below. In the open window stands Dr. Alucard holding a pistol he has just fired. He smiles at you.

"A silver bullet," he explains. "It is the only way to kill a werewolf."

You begin to say thanks, but all that comes out of your mouth is an animal-like growl. You look at your hands in disbelief. Tiny hairs are growing all over them! The werewolf is dead, but he lived long enough to spread his dreadful disease to you! Don't worry. It'll be a cause of embarrassment for you only a few days every month. Happy howling!

THE END

You shake your head at the Monster and say, "Nothing doing." This does not please him. He gnashes his teeth and snarls viciously at you. His eyes burn with hate. He doesn't look sweet anymore!

You think you are safe from his fury, but suddenly he pulls violently at his chains and one of them tears away from the ancient wall. With a cry of triumph, he pulls on the other chain and it begins to loosen.

You decide you have tarried long enough in the basement. You race for the stairs. But as you reach the door, you hear footsteps above. It is Alucard coming down to look for you! Trapped!

Don't just stand there! Your only hope is to turn to PAGE 92.

You leave the room and continue down the darkened hall. Suddenly a low voice speaks behind you. "And just *where* do you think *you're* going?"

You spin around, but there is no one there. Not even a shadow.

"Well, aren't you going to say something?" it asks again.

"But where are you?" you ask fearfully. "I can't see you!"

"Of course you can't," replies the voice. "Who has ever seen the Invisible Man?"

"Invisible?" you sputter.

"That's right," says the voice, drawing nearer. "Don't get the idea I *wanted* to be invisible. It was all Alucard's idea. He used me as his guinea pig in his experiments. At first I was invisible for just a few hours. But then he gave me more and more of the invisible drug, and I was invisible for longer periods. Now I'm afraid I'll never be visible again. Unless I can find the formula for visibility."

"That's terrible," you reply. "I wish I could help you. But I'm as much a prisoner here as you are."

The voice seems right next to you now. "Oh, but you can help me," says the Invisible Man. All at once five icy fingers, invisible but very real, close in around your throat. "You *are* going to help me!!"

Flip over to PAGE 49 while you still can.

"You—you have saved me," says the girl.

"Who are you and what are you doing here?" you ask.

"My name's Terry. I came here to interview Alucard for the school newspaper. He drugged me and made me his prisoner. I've been locked up here for weeks."

"But why? What does he want with either of us?"

"Our blood," whispers Terry. "Spell Alucard backwards and what do you get?"

"Dracula!" you cry. "You mean to say he's a . . . vampire?"

"The original vampire," explains your new friend. "He needs our blood to survive—but that's not the worst part! Soon I will turn into a vampire myself. And so will you, unless we stop him!"

"But how?" you ask.

"He's defenseless during the daylight hours," Terry tells you. "At dawn he must return to his coffin and sleep till nightfall. I know a secret passageway through the library. We'll find him and destroy him while he sleeps!"

Terry stretches out a hand to you. It is cold and you shiver at its touch.

If you trust Terry, turn to PAGE 51.

If you are unsure of your new friend and want to call your own shots, turn to PAGE 60.

44

You step behind the heavy metal door you have just passed through. You hear Frankenstein's Monster approaching. Slowly—but very surely—his heavy footsteps head toward you. You pray the monster won't find you! If only your heart wasn't pounding so loudly.

Suddenly the Monster enters the room, swinging the door back to the wall with one mighty push of his powerful arm. Splat! You are flattened into a human pancake. You'd go great with syrup, if they can ever peel you off the wall.

THE END

Your new acquaintance flings his head back and begins to howl at the moon. You jump back to the other side of the roof and wait for the terrible transformation to begin. But nothing happens. He continues to howl, but doesn't grow a single hair on his body.

"Some werewolf," you say to yourself. You're a little ashamed you were afraid of him at all. You leave the man to his howling and cross the roof to find some way to get down to the ground and your car.

When you circle to the back of the mansion, you see a strange sight below on the back lawn. Alucard and Igor are carrying a coffin toward a small graveyard behind the house. What are they up to?

If you want to investigate further, turn to PAGE 54.

If getting out of there is more important to you, turn to PAGE 59.

You fling open the closet door and rush out. You look to the right—then to the left. Igor is not in sight. So far, so good.

You race to the main staircase and plunge down the stairs. Your heart pounds with fear. There are three flights to the first floor. You make it down in Olympic-record time.

You reach the front hallway. You're almost out the door. You turn the huge brass doorknob as quietly as you can. But before you can make your escape, there is a loud knock at the front door. You step back in surprise. Who could it be?

Hold your breath and turn to PAGE 18.

You're not going to stick around to find out what kind of creep is waiting in the shadows. You open the nearest window and step into a darkened bedroom. You feel your way to the light switch on the wall.

The first sight that greets your eyes is a teenaged girl tied to a chair. The stranger has bright red hair and the greenest eyes you've ever seen.

"Help me," she says weakly. "Get me out of here before he comes back."

You don't have to think twice to figure out who "he" is. You undo the ropes and the girl stands up stiffly.

Turn to PAGE 43

48

You take a deep breath and raise Igor's punch to your lips. You swallow some of the foul-smelling drink. It tastes like a mixture of stale ginger ale and swamp water. Your first reaction is to spit it out. But Igor is watching you intently. You finish swallowing and force yourself to smile.

"Delicious," you say.

Igor says something, but you can't make it out. His voice sounds strangely far away and muffled. The room is beginning to spin around you. You drop the glass, but you don't hear it break. You put your hand on the chair to steady yourself. The room is spinning faster and faster. Suddenly everything goes black.

If your favorite soda is ginger ale, turn to PAGE 25.

If you prefer cola, turn to PAGE 32.

"Sure!" you manage to blurt out. The icy invisible fingers relax their grip on your throat and an invisible hand shoves you forward.

"Move," orders the Invisible Man.

You consider making a break for it. But how do you escape from an enemy you can't see?

The Invisible Man takes you into Alucard's laboratory. Before you is a table covered with beakers and test tubes of different-colored concoctions.

"I want you to drink from each of these beakers," says your captor. "One of them is sure to be the liquid that will make me visible again."

"But how will that help?" you ask. "After all, I'm not invisible, am I?"

"No," he replies, "but if any of those liquids contain poison, I'll know which to avoid, won't I? Now start drinking!"

With a sick feeling in your stomach, you realize you are to be his guinea pig! You look down at the table. The two nearest beakers contain a purple liquid and a green liquid. Which will it be first? Decide fast. The Invisible Man is getting impatient!

If you decide to reach for the purple liquid, turn to PAGE 63.

If you decide to go for the green liquid, turn to PAGE 85.

Remaining in the closet is torture, but getting caught again by Igor and his Master is even less appealing. Your companion in the closet makes no further move. Unable to stand the fear of the unknown any longer, you remove a book of matches from your pocket and light one. The flame flickers on the face of a tall man with gray hair. His skin is well tanned and all he wears is a loincoth. Despite his glowing eyes, he seems to be more dead than alive. It suddenly occurs to you that he may well be dead—a walking zombie!

The light and warmth of the match have a strange effect on the zombie. His mouth opens and be begins to speak in a low, dull voice. "What will my Master have me do?" he asks.

The flame has activated him and he has mistaken you for his Master. Your mind whirls as you try to think of something to say.

If you want to command the zombie to get you out of the mansion, turn to PAGE 57.

If you want to command him to go back to sleep, turn to PAGE 61.

"All right," you say to your friend. "Lead the way."

Terry takes you down the darkened hall to the library. The walls are crowded with hundreds of books. Your companion takes one large, dusty volume off a shelf. As the book is removed, the shelves begin to revolve, revealing a secret passageway.

"Come on," says Terry.

Suddenly you hear footsteps behind you. "Stop!" cries a voice from the doorway. You turn to see who it is. Dumb move. The bookshelves are beginning to revolve back to their original position. Your friend has replaced the book on the shelf and is already through the passageway, but you won't make it. You look at the books on the shelf. The right one will open the shelves again. But which book is it?

If you pull out Tales of Terror, turn to PAGE 80.

If you pull out Rebecca of Sunnybrook Farm, turn to PAGE 71.

You turn back to face your friend on the roof. You notice that hair is growing on his face and hands. "It's already started!" cries the poor fellow.

You stare in frozen horror as hair sprouts like weeds all over his body. With long, jagged fingernails, he tears open his shirt to reveal a chest covered with thick brown animal hair. He snarls and growls and bends down into a crouched position, ready to spring at you. You step back and nearly fall off the roof. You glance down fearfully at the ground below. It's a long drop and you could break your legs, but that may be preferable to staying on the roof and facing the werewolf! You might be able to climb in the window to the room you just left, but it's halfway around the roof. You may not be able to get there before the werewolf attacks!

If you decide to jump, turn to PAGE 36.
If you decide to try for the open window, turn to PAGE 40.

54

You are anxious to know who—or what—Alucard and Igor have in the coffin. As quietly as possible, you climb down the thick ivy that grows on the back wall of the mansion. You drop to the ground with a thud, but Alucard and Igor are too far away to hear the noise.

You creep across the backyard to the small cemetery. To find out what the two are doing, you plan a diversion.

"Ooooooooowwwww!" you cry from behind a thick bush, imitating the howling of your wolfish friend on the roof.

"What was that?" says Igor with a start.

"Oh, it's probably that new patient," replies Alucard. "You know how he gets when there's a full moon."

"It doesn't sound like him," says Igor. "I'd know his howl anywhere."

"Go take a look then," suggests his Master.

"Not me," says the servant. "You go."

In disgust, Alucard takes one of their two lanterns and begins to walk in your direction.

"Who is there?" he calls out.

Go on to PAGE 79.

You've got to help Frankie. You rush forward and grab Igor's hand, twisting it as hard as you can. He cries out in pain and drops the torch. It clatters to the cave floor and sputters in a small pool of water.

Frankie roars and comes toward Igor. The hunchback runs screaming down the passageway. But the Monster does not pursue him. There is someone else whom he hates much more—Dr. Alucard. With burning eyes he turns on his creator.

"Get back!" commands Alucard. "I am your Master!"

"You hurt me," says Frankie. "You chained me like a slave."

The doctor is losing his cool. "Yes, but I was going to let you go," he stammers. "Don't you realize I was about to give you a new brain?" He turns and points to you. "I was going to take this one's brain and put it into your body. I still can if you'll only let me!"

But Frankie isn't buying it. He reaches out for Alucard with those huge, green hands. Before he can grasp the doctor, Alucard pulls his cape around himself and changes into a tiny bat!

If you think bats are neat animals, turn to PAGE 62.

If you rate bats slightly below snakes, turn to PAGE 65.

As you pull down the lever, a trap door springs open beneath your feet and you plunge down into the unknown. You are knocked unconscious by your fall.

When you come to, you are sitting on wet grass. You look around in astonishment. You are outside the mansion. The trap door was an escape hatch to freedom!

You pick yourself up and stumble to your car in the driveway. You get in and speed away. You don't stop until you reach an all-night gas station.

While your tank is being filled, you call the police and tell them about the mansion, Alucard, and Terry, who is still inside and possibly in danger.

You hang up and climb back into your car. You wonder how you will explain your lateness to your worried parents. You begin practicing your excuse as you drive. "Dad," you say, "I know you're not going to believe this, but . . ."

THE END

"Get me out of here!" you command. At the sound of your voice, the zombie opens the closet door and pushes you out in front of him.

"Hey, take it easy!" you cry. But before you can say another word, Igor comes down the hallway toward you. He ignores the zombie and grabs you in both arms. It is a fatal mistake on his part. The zombie pulls Igor off you and lifts him up into the air with both hands. Then he tosses the hunchback down the hall like a sack of potatoes. Igor hits the wall and lands in a heap on the floor. He doesn't move.

Alucard appears at the head of the stairs. He tries to counteract your command, but the zombie has a one-track mind. Unlike Igor, the doctor doesn't come between you and the zombie. He knows better than to mess with his own monster.

Outside the mansion, you try to start up your car, but there's not enough gas left. That's no problem, however, when you have a helpful zombie in your power. He lifts you up on his muscular shoulders and carries you piggyback to the nearest bus station. Your parents aren't going to be too crazy about having your new "friend" move in with you, but your friends at school will sure be impressed.

THE END

The engine revs loudly, and you shift into drive. The car doesn't move.

"What's the matter now?" cries Chris, as Igor circles around to the front of the car, waving his club menacingly.

"I don't know!" you exclaim. You fumble madly with all the dials and knobs on the dashboard. In your frenzy, you turn on the windshield wipers, the radio, and the air conditioner. But still the car won't move.

Igor is right on top of you now. He has climbed onto the hood of the car. He raises his club up over his head.

All at once you look down and realize you have forgotten to release the emergency brake. As you reach down to do this, Igor brings his club down on the windshield. Smash! It shatters into a thousand pieces.

He reaches into the car with a large, hairy hand and grasps you by the throat. It looks as if you're not going anywhere tonight after all!

THE END

You'd rather beat it than find out what Alucard and Igor are up to this time. You find a drainpipe on the side of the house. Holding on for dear life, you begin to shinny down it slowly. But the pipe is old and your weight is more than it can hold. It breaks off the house and comes crashing down to the ground. You might have survived if you'd landed on the soft, wet grass. But, unfortunately, your head hits an ancient tombstone on the edge of the graveyard. Thus this story comes to a painful end.

Rest In Peace

60

You pull your hand away from the girl.

"I'm sorry," you say to Terry, "but I'm not interested in getting revenge. I just want to get out of this house alive. I wish you luck, but it's not my fight."

Terry looks disappointed, but accepts your decision.

As you turn toward the door, she says, "Here, take this. You may need it if you run into Alucard again."

Your friend places a long, sharp, wooden stake into your hand. You look at it in surprise.

"I secretly sharpened it in my room during the day while Alucard slept in his coffin," explains Terry. "If he should attack you, plunge it into his heart and it will destroy him."

You grasp the stake tightly in your hand. "But how will you defend yourself?" you ask.

Terry pulls out another stake from a belt. "I made two," she says with a strange smile. "Just in case."

Turn to PAGE 67.

"Go to sleep!" you say to the zombie.

Unfortunately, you are not used to ordering around the walking dead. The zombie thinks you want him to put you to sleep. Before you can straighten things out, he lifts both powerful hands and brings them down together on your head. The idea is to knock you unconscious. But the zombie doesn't know his own strength. The blow puts a sizable dent in your skull and you sink to the floor of the closet, never to awaken again. Nighty, night, and sweet dreams!

THE END

62

The vampire bat dives for Frankie's thick, green neck. The Monster screams and sinks to his knees. The bat swirls back into the air and up the passageway toward the mansion. Frankie moans. Bright red drops of blood drip from his injured neck.

You give your friend a handkerchief to stop the flow of blood and take his hand. "Come on," you say, "let's get out of here while we still can." He follows you, and together you make your way to the end of the passageway.

You both step out into the fresh night air on a hillside some distance from the mansion. Afraid to go back for your car, you and Frankie walk down to a pay phone. You call the police and they pick you up in a squad car. But when you arrive at the mansion again, Alucard and Igor are gone. The vampire has escaped to strike again. Dracula still lives. But so do you. And that is enough to make you feel happy and relieved . . . for the moment.

THE END

You raise the beaker filled with the purple liquid to your lips and drink. It tastes chalky and bitter. Suddenly you notice something strange. Your hand holding the beaker is slowly fading from sight!

"You're turning into . . . ME!" the Invisible Man exclaims.

It's true. The purple liquid has made you invisible, too.

You start running for the laboratory door. As you rush down the hall to the staircase you can hear the Invisible Man's footsteps behind you. He still has one advantage over you. He has no clothes on to outline his body and you do. Quickly, you begin pulling off your clothes as you descend the staircase. Shirt . . . jeans . . . shoes. By the time you reach the front door you are completely naked and completely invisible.

You hop into your car with a laugh and drive off, leaving the Invisible Man and the other monsters of Monster Mansion behind. You wonder how you're going to gas up without causing a panic. But even more important, you wonder if the purple liquid will keep you invisible until you're safely home. You don't particularly want to get caught in public with your pants down!

THE END

"Two plus two is four," you reply.

"Good!" smiles the doctor. You smile back. Maybe this is a test, and if you get everything right he'll let you go. He proceeds to ask you a number of other questions about science, math, history, and English. You answer every one correctly.

"Excellent!" exclaims Alucard. "I applaud you on your intelligence. I think we can get started with the operation."

"But—but aren't you going to let me go?" you stammer.

Igor laughs cruelly. "Oh, I'm afraid I couldn't do that," explains the doctor. "Now that I know the superior quality of your brain, I'm going to transfer it to my creature."

Igor pulls a white sheet off a figure lying nearby on another table. The creature's green skin and square head are all too familiar—Frankenstein's Monster!

If you had only known. You let out a scream of terror, but it is useless. Alucard takes a sharp silver scalpel from Igor and the operation begins. In a few hours it is all over. The experiment is a success. You may not look so hot anymore in your new green body, but look on the bright side. You'll never have to worry about the school bully pushing you around again!

THE END

The bat flaps its long, black wings and flies down the narrow passageway you yourself just thought of taking.

Frankie runs after it, howling with anger. Unwittingly, the Monster walks right into a pit of quicksand. He slowly sinks down into the wet sand. The bat hovers above his head, rejoicing over the Monster's doom.

But Frankie has not given up the chase. With one last powerful lunge he reaches up and grabs the bat in his green hands. The animal screeches as the Monster crumples it between his powerful fingers. Frankie sinks down to his shoulders, still holding the remains of what was once Alucard in his hands.

You try to do something to save Frankie, but it is too late. Just before his head goes under, he turns his sad eyes on you and smiles. You turn away, unable to look. You sadly head down the passageway to freedom.

THE END

"You shouldn't have done that to my coffin," says the vampire.

Sunlight is flooding the cellar floor. To reach you, Dracula must step out of the shadows and into the light.

"What are you going to do about it?" you shoot back.

Dracula comes forward, stepping directly into the sunlight. He continues to advance.

"I—I don't understand," you stammer fearfully. "The sunlight—it was supposed to destroy you!"

Dracula grins, revealing a mouthful of sharp fangs.

"I'm afraid you've been watching too many old movies," he says. They are the last words you will ever hear.

THE END

You wish Terry good luck and cautiously sneak out into the hallway once more. From the staircase you listen for the sound of voices. All is still. You go down to the main floor and cross the hall where the fireplace is still glowing. The front door remains locked—you must try to find another that is open. Suddenly you hear footsteps coming down the stairs. Where can you hide?

If you go into the dining room, turn to PAGE 70.

If you go into the kitchen, turn to PAGE 74.

"I suppose it *is* our duty to stop Alucard's plan," you say. "Lead the way."

Chris takes you up a rickety, narrow staircase to the attic and a large room with a skylight. Test tubes and glass beakers filled with brightly colored chemicals line one wall. In the center of the room is a raised platform with a crank.

"That's where Alucard will raise the Monster to revive him with lightning from the storm," explains Chris.

"That is correct, Chris," says a familiar voice from across the room. "Too bad neither of you will be around to see it." You both turn and stare into the smiling face of Dr. Alucard. Igor is blocking the door you just came through.

"So you two have met, eh?" says the doctor. "How very nice! It is only proper since you will soon be sharing an operating table."

"Run!" Chris cries. And you do. But the only place to run to is a wall. You bump into two switches. One is red and the other is blue.

"Pull the switch!" cries your friend. "It shuts off the lights!"

Fine, you think to yourself. But which is the right switch?

If you pull the red switch, turn to PAGE 73.

If you pull the blue, turn to PAGE 81.

You lunge forward and grasp the necklace around Alucard's neck. You give it a strong tug and it breaks off in your hand. You hold up the gold charm before Karla, the Mummy. His hand reaches up for it. With a forceful swing, you heave the charm out the half-opened window into the darkness.

"Go get it, Karla!" you cry.

The obedient Mummy dives through the window and plunges to the ground below.

You turn to face Alucard, but he is no longer there. All that remains of him is a pile of ashes on the floor. Apparently he needed the charm more than Karla did. You are now the Master of Monster Mansion.

THE END

You quickly step into an elegant dining room. Bad choice. At the end of a long banquet table sits Count Dracula.

"Ah, my friend!" he cries, rising to his feet. "I was beginning to wonder what had become of you."

You quickly hide the sharpened wooden stake behind your back. The door opens and Igor enters.

"I'm afraid you are a little late for the main course," apologizes the Count. "But you are just in time for dessert."

"No thanks," you mumble, backing away. "I'm not hungry."

Igor begins to laugh hysterically at this remark.

"What's so funny?" you ask.

"You must excuse Igor," says Dracula. "He has a morbid sense of humor. You see, I wasn't inviting you to *eat* dessert. You, my dear young friend, *are* dessert. But don't be alarmed. We will need only about a pint of your blood to make the blood pudding truly delicious!"

Igor twists the stake out of your hand and begins dragging you toward the kitchen. This makes you very mad! "You guys really make my blood boil!" you shout.

"Who told you the recipe?" asks Igor in surprise.

Don't look now—this is really . . .

THE END

Good guess! You didn't go for the obvious choice! As you pull out *Rebecca of Sunnybrook Farm*, the opening between the shelves widens.

You rush into the passageway and the bookshelves close behind you. You call out for your friend in the darkness of the passageway. There is no answer. Terry has gone on without you. You stumble forward, having no idea where the passageway will lead. You feel along the wall until your hand touches a long, wooden lever. What can you lose by pulling it?

Turn to PAGE 56 and hope for the best.

72

This time, the engine starts up like a dream. You floor the gas pedal and the car shoots down the driveway, throwing gravel into the air.

You look into the rearview mirror at Igor. He is jumping up and down, beating his club on the driveway. You can't help laughing at the sight of him.

"What's so funny?" asks Chris.

You are laughing too hard to answer.

THE END

Too bad! Wrong switch!

The red switch sets off a charge of dynamite under the foundation of the mansion. It blows the entire building sky high, laboratory and all. Happy landing!

THE END

You quickly duck into the large, old-fashioned kitchen. Onions and garlic hang from the ceiling. In one corner is a big wood-burning stove. A bubbling kettle sits on top of the stove, and a big silver soup spoon lies on the sideboard. You crouch down behind the stove as a shadow falls across the kitchen floor. You try to stay hidden, but Alucard has already seen you.

"You shouldn't be down here, my friend," he says softly.

"I want to leave *now*, Count Dracula!" you say firmly.

"So you know my real name," says the Count. "That is most unfortunate." This time when he smiles his sharp fangs shine in the light of the full moon. He comes still closer, his wild eyes fixed on your neck.

If you reach for your wooden stake, turn to PAGE 76.

If you try to attack him with the silver spoon, turn to PAGE 90.

If you grab the garlic to ward him off, turn to PAGE 78.

You push Alucard out of your way and pull open the door. Karla is too slow to react and Alucard is taken completely by surprise. You run for your life down the hall. But you realize that if you keep running, they'll quickly catch up again. You'd better hide. You tear open a door to a room and duck inside. You wait, holding your breath, until Alucard and the Mummy pass by. When all is quiet again, you slowly open the door.

Turn to PAGE 42.

You pull the wooden stake from your belt and stab at Dracula with it. The vampire lets out a cry of rage and pulls away unhurt. He gathers his cape tightly around him. Before your startled eyes he transforms himself into a bat. Your stake is useless against the small flying creature. The bat flaps its wings and flies toward the open cellar door.

But it is not only your pointed stake that has driven Dracula to retreat. You see the first rays of morning fall across the kitchen floor. The vampire is racing to return to his tomb before the light reaches him!

Turn to PAGE 84, and step on it!

You recall from your old movie viewing how garlic is something vampires can't stand, and you pull down a string of the stuff from the ceiling. You realize it would be more effective to use your stake, but you can't bring yourself to use it—not even on Dracula.

You hold up the garlic in front of the vampire's eyes. He shrinks back in terror at the sight of it, pulling his cape up to his face.

"Beat it, Dracula," you say, filled with self-confidence, "before I make you eat this stuff!"

Hissing loudly, Dracula rushes out of the kitchen. You drop the garlic with a sigh of relief. Suddenly from the next room comes a blood-curdling scream! A moment later Terry enters the kitchen. In her hand is the wooden stake. Drops of bright-red blood drip from its sharpened point onto the floor.

"I just ran into a friend of ours," says Terry quietly. "It is over. Dracula is dead."

THE END

As Alucard draws closer to your hiding place, you stealthily creep around him in a circle until you are very near to the gravesite. Igor is looking out into the darkness, waiting anxiously for Alucard's return. The shovel is on the ground beside him. You quietly lift it up. The hunchback whirls around to face you, but not soon enough. You bash him squarely over the head with the shovel. He drops to the ground, unconscious.

You bend down to the simple, wooden coffin next to the open grave and lift the lid. Inside is an attractive girl your own age, dressed all in white. The moonlight shines on her pale face and the girl's eyes open.

"Who are you?" she asks in surprise.

"There's no time now for introductions," you whisper. "We've got to get out of here before Alucard comes back."

As you help the stranger from the coffin, the girl leaps at you. You scream as her white fangs find your jugular vein. Too late, you learn the truth of the old saying: "Let sleeping vampires lie."

THE END

Oops! Wrong book! *Tales of Terror* is too obvious!

The bookshelves continue to close. You try to squeeze through the opening, but it's too small. If you hadn't had so many hot-fudge sundaes this month, you might have been thin enough to make it!

You look at the person who spoke from the doorway. It is Dr. Alucard. He watches and smiles as the heavy bookshelves crush the life out of you.

THE END

The lights go off! You are lost in the darkness. Someone cries out and you feel a hand take yours and pull you across the floor. In a few moments you are in the hallway. Chris, who is holding your hand, lets go of it. Together you run down the staircase and out the front door.

Your car is still sitting in the gravel driveway. You fumble in your pocket for the keys.

"Hurry!" cries Chris.

You find the keys and open both doors. As you slip the key in the ignition, you see Igor bounding out the front door of the mansion. You turn the key, but the engine won't start!

"What's the matter?" asks Chris, sounding very nervous.

"It's low on gas," you explain and try to start the car again. Igor is coming straight for you with a large wooden club and he means business.

If you know something about cars, turn to PAGE 72.

If you don't know a stick shift from an emergency brake, turn to PAGE 58.

You just want to get out of this creepy mansion! "I'm sorry, but it's too risky," you insist.

Chris sees you don't want to bother destroying Alucard's Monster. "All right," your friend says reluctantly. "We'll do it your way. Let's get out of here."

The two of you sneak out of the room and down the stairs. You get out the front door without being seen and jump into your car.

There's just enough gas left in the tank to get you to a police station five miles down the road. The two of you tell the officer on duty your amazing story. He seems doubtful, but agrees to send a squad car out to investigate Alucard's mansion.

The police discover Alucard's laboratory and the remains of several "guests" used in his experiments. The mad doctor and his servant are arrested for murder, and the mansion is closed down. You and Chris are heroes! When your mother sees your picture on the front page of the morning paper, she actually waits two minutes before yelling at you for staying out late, not cleaning your room, and forgetting your homework.

THE END

You run down the stairs—directly into the arms of Igor!

"There you are!" cries the hunchback. "I was just about to come get you. The Master is waiting. Dinner is ready."

Dinner? Is this another trick? You have little time to think it over as Igor escorts you into the dining room.

"Ah! My friend!" exclaims Dr. Alucard. "I am so sorry that you are a bit under the weather . . . but we tried to make you comfortable until the effects wore off."

You mumble something in reply, unable to trust your host or anything he says.

"I've called the local garage and someone should be here shortly to see to your car," continues Alucard. "In the meantime, I insist you join me for dinner."

You sit down and think that maybe your host isn't such a bad guy after all. Igor places a soup plate in front of you. It looks weird and has a funny smell.

"It's homemade spider soup," explains the hunchback proudly. "I made it myself. Eat it before it cools. But save room for the salamander casserole. It's my specialty."

You force a smile and pick up your spoon. It wouldn't do at all to insult your host and his cook. And you know what? The spider soup really isn't too bad!

THE END

84

You bound down the cellar stairs after the bat. There, in a dark corner, is a large coffin partly filled with soil. It must be from his home in Transylvania, you decide. The bat dives for your head, but you brush it away before it can bite you.

You lift the heavy coffin with both hands and turn it over. It crashes to the floor, spilling the soil everywhere. The bat shrieks loudly and transforms itself back into Dracula. There is a look of murder in his eyes.

Will you defeat him? You will with luck. Flip a coin.

Heads—turn to PAGE 66.
Tails—turn to PAGE 24.

You gulp down the green, bubbling liquid from the beaker. It doesn't taste bad at all—sort of sweet, but tangy. It makes your body tingle from your head to your toes. As you finish the potion, you hear the Invisible Man scream. You listen as his footsteps go rushing toward the door and out into the hallway.

What could have frightened him? You glance in the large laboratory mirror and give a scream yourself. You're quite a sight. Hair is growing out all over your face. Your teeth are growing into sharp fangs. Foam is bubbling out of your mouth. You look like Mr. Hyde with a bad case of rabies. Darn that green liquid anyway!

It is easy to make your escape now. But, oddly enough, the urge to leave has left you. Now that you're a monster, you feel right at home in Monster Mansion. And why shouldn't you?

THE END

You decide to wait for a better chance to escape. Igor continues to roll your bed to the end of the corridor. There is a metal door on the wall in front of you. The hunchback opens it and tips the bed up. Before you know what's happening, you slide off the bed and down a long, dark chute. Down, down, down you slide. Maybe at the bottom of the chute is freedom. More likely you will end up in a cell in a dungeon, you think.

You are wrong on both counts. Your final destination is a garbage dump. You spend two smelly days there, but make your escape when the trash is taken away.

Not a very dignified ending, but still a happy one.

THE END

You pass the driveway and continue down the road in the pouring rain. You wonder how many more miles you can cover before the car conks out. Suddenly, you see a sign by the roadside. It says: GAS AND FOOD—ONE MILE AHEAD. You breathe a deep sigh of relief and think how smart you were not to stop at that old mansion. As you dream about the juicy cheeseburger and chocolate shake you are going to order when you stop, you round a sharp curve and skid head-on into a ten-ton truck coming the other way. Too bad you'll never taste that cheeseburger!

THE END

The terrible colors from the screen seem to be swirling around in your head. Your body is swaying from side to side. You feel Alucard taking your hand in his warm one.

"Come, my friend," he says gently. "You don't look well. Perhaps you should lie down for a while."

You want to say you're not his friend, but you can't seem to get your lips to form the words. Instead you nod tipsily as he leads you from the den to a hall where a long staircase looms darkly before you. That is the last thing you remember before you lose consciousness.

Turn to PAGE 25. Fast!

You decide not to wait around to see who the mysterious footsteps belong to. So you climb out the window and onto the roof. It is made of old wooden shingles that are cracked and broken. You walk carefully, watching your balance and avoiding the broken shingles. If you slip on one, it could be the end of you.

As you approach the edge of the roof, you suddenly stop short. There, against the moonlight, is the shadow of a person! It seems you are not alone on this roof. Could it be Igor or Alucard looking for you?

You make a nervous movement. Your foot kicks a shingle loose. It slides off the roof and clatters on the ground below. The shadow turns quickly at the noise. It's moving toward you! What now?

If you want to see who the shadow belongs to, turn to PAGE 26.

If you'd rather not know and want to take your chances back inside, turn to PAGE 47.

You remember seeing a werewolf killed in an old movie by being beaten over the head with a silver cane. You figure what's good for a werewolf ought to work on a vampire as well. You seize the silver soup spoon from the sideboard and pull it back over your head. You bring it down with all your strength on Alucard's skull. The spoon is bent in half, but the vampire's hair isn't even mussed.

As Alucard laughs, you turn over the spoon and read the words printed on it: IMITATION SILVER. It is the last thing you see as the fangs sink into your neck.

THE END

The Monster's large, dark eyes stare up at you in pain. "Help me," he groans. The Monster is terrifying, yet there is something strangely sweet about this big green guy. He points a finger toward the corner. There you see a key hanging from a nail on the wall. From the look in his eyes, you know it will unlock the manacles.

If you want to unlock the Monster's chains, turn to PAGE 27.

If you want to leave him right where he is, turn to PAGE 41.

In the darkness you hear the Monster's growls coming toward you. He is free! You stumble back through an open doorway leading into another section of the basement. To the left, you hear the sound of lapping water. There must be a pool of water here. Perhaps it is fed by an underground stream—a stream that could carry you out of the mansion and to freedom. The Monster's heavy footsteps are drawing nearer out of the darkness.

If you decide to dive into the pool, turn to PAGE 16.

If you decide to hide behind the door and let the Monster pass you, turn to PAGE 44.

Suddenly you don't feel so well.

"He's told me his whole mad scheme," continues Chris. "As soon as he finds the proper brain to go with my heart, Alucard's going to start operating. And I have a feeling you've been elected."

"I'm not all that smart," you say, suddenly wishing you were a lot dumber.

"The only way to stop him is for us to get into the laboratory and destroy everything," says your new friend. "Now that you've freed me from this room we can do it, together."

You shake your head. "I think we should just worry about getting out of this place alive," you say. "Once we're safe, we can tell the police everything. They'll be able to handle Alucard a lot better than we could."

"No!" exclaims Chris. "We've got to stop him *now!*"

If you go along with Chris's plan, turn to PAGE 68.

If you insist on getting out of the mansion first, turn to PAGE 82.

Collect All the Twistaplot® Books

Your collection won't be complete without:
#14 *Instant Millionaire* by R. L. Stine
You have just won a million dollars! But wait, there's
a catch. You have a month to spend the money or
you lose it. Think it will be fun to spend a million
bucks? Think it will be easy? You'll see.